SOARING

MARY LYNN MICHELLE

In loving memory of Edward Royce,
my fun-loving uncle who always encouraged my writing.

A special thanks to Katrina Byrd for writing the song.

1

There's always a beginning, middle, and an end to a story, but don't you think there's more to life than just that. I always dreamed of riding a racehorse and winning the race, and my dream finally came true.

It all began when I went on an end-of-the-year school field trip with my two best friends to a stable. There I got my wish of finally being a jockey. My friends also won a race, but I learned that there's more to life than just winning. I learned that all from Silver Dash, who taught me that dreams can come true.

But I am getting ahead of myself; the story begins at school.

*****

At Willow Brook Middle School, Aliyah, Josh, and I were heading to class on Monday to get ready for the field trip. It was going to be a one-week field trip to Crest Hill Stables—that's a half day's drive from our school—then we drive back on Sunday. That gave us almost a full week to be with the horses.

Crest Hill Stables is a famous racetrack that holds a Championship Cup each year for the chance to win a very large amount of money from investors who bet on the winning horse. The winner of the race gets the prize money that is announced at the end of the race, depending on the bets, and the rest goes to the stables. It helps to keep the races going each year, but I had heard from the news on television that the stables were having financial trouble. Everyone was starting to worry if it was going to close down soon. That's why this was such an exciting trip since no one knows if it will be open next year for another race.

Oh, I'm Sara, by the way. I have long curly light-brown hair that goes to my back, with pale skin. I like to wear blue jeans, light-green shirts, and white sneakers. I have light-brown eyes like my hair, wear brown-trimmed glasses, and I like to wear long gold-colored earrings. Aliyah and Josh, whom I told you about earlier, are my two best friends.

Aliyah has curly short black hair that ends at her shoulders, and she has a really pretty light-brown skin tone. She likes to wear blue jeans, lavender shirts, which really brings out her skin tone nicely, and lavender sneakers. She likes to wear black sunglasses, so you can't see her eyes, but her eyes are dark brown, almost as dark as her hair. She also likes to wear medium silver hoop earrings. She's a little silly and likes to act things out a lot with her hands, but we are best friends; in fact, you can say that we're more like sisters. We hang out all the time, we like the same stuff, and we even finish each other's sentences.

Finally, there's Josh. He has a fun-loving attitude and is always late to class. He has a little darker pale skin tone than I do and short brown hair, likes to wear blue jeans, red shirts, and red sneakers. He has brown eyes a little darker than his hair. He always makes me laugh, and I have a secret crush on him, but he doesn't know that. Of course, Aliyah knows about my crush; we tell each other everything. I'm waiting for Josh to say that he likes me first before I tell him.

Aliyah and I were already in class, and you guessed it—Josh was late again. The bell rang, and Mrs. Colswerth was going through attendance. She's our history teacher who's tall and thin, has a darker brown skin tone than Aliyah, short black straight hair that ends at her shoulders, and likes to wear green clothing almost all the time. She has light-brown eyes.

"Brittney?" Mrs. Colswerth yelled out.

"Here," Brittney yelled back.

"Johnny?" Mrs. Colswerth said.

"Here," Johnny yelled back.

"Sara?" Mrs. Colswerth yelled.

"Here," I yelled back.

Then Josh came rushing through the door, and everyone stared at him. He was breathing deeply and looked a little sweaty since he was running.

"You're late again," Mrs. Colswerth said with annoyance.

"Sorry, I won't be late again—I promise," Josh said, still breathing deeply.

"I'll believe that when I see it. Now go sit down," Mrs. Colswerth said, and everyone chuckled.

"Where were you, Josh?" I asked when he sat next to me.

"I was with my friends," he answered.

"Your friends?" I asked.

"Couldn't your friends be closer to class for once?" Aliyah asked, and I giggled.

"They're in the other hall," Josh answered, and everyone started to laugh harder.

"Well, that helps," Aliyah said sarcastically, and everyone laughed even more now, including me.

"That's enough, you two. Class, settle down. I have something important to say. When we get on the bus, we are going to stop for lunch during the trip. Does everyone have money and extra clothes for the trip?" Mrs. Colswerth asked the class.

"Yes, Mrs. Colswerth," everyone in the class answered.

"Good. It looks like everyone is here, so go out to the bus," Mrs. Colswerth said, looking at the attendance again.

Everyone got up and headed for the bus with their luggage. The bus was one of those big double-sized busses that are for long drives that usually has a bathroom at the end of it. It's a dark-blue color with a black trim, and when I got close to it, all I smelled was the exhaust.

The bus driver was there, waiting for everyone. He's a bit bigger in the middle section, with curly brown hair and wearing a bus driver's blue cargo pants and short-sleeve shirt with a blue cap that had the name of the bus we were riding on—THE CREST HILL EXPRESS. He put our luggage in a storage space near the bottom of the bus.

Aliyah, Josh, and I were the first ones to get on the bus. Aliyah and I went in a three seater, and Josh went in a two seater. We sat in the second seat from the front because Aliyah and I let Mrs. Colswerth sit in the front, and Josh liked to hang out with us, so he sat across from us.

"I can't wait to get to the stables," Aliyah said with excitement.

"Me either," I said.

"This is going to be a lot of fun. Don't you think so too, Josh?" Aliyah asked.

"Yeah, this is going to be great," he answered back.

"Just please don't try to hurt the horses or scare them, okay?" I insisted.

"Don't worry, I won't," he answered with a shrug.

I give him a stern look, and Aliyah started to giggle. Everyone was still coming onto the bus, and I was near the window because I usually like to daydream.

"Okay, okay. I promise I won't startle them," Josh finally admitted.

I give him a smile and turned to look out the window. When I looked out, I saw Mrs. Colswerth talking to another teacher. Mrs. Colswerth looked upset for some reason, and by the time she was done talking with the other teacher, everyone was on the bus and ready to go. Mrs. Colswerth came on, and I wanted to ask her what was wrong.

"Hi, Mrs. Colswerth. What's the matter?" I asked curiously.

"Oh, it's one of the students," she answered with a tired tone of voice.

"What's wrong?" Aliyah asked. It seemed Aliyah was wondering the same thing I was.

"The student turned up really sick, and I had to take him off the trip list," Mrs. Colswerth answered.

"So what's wrong with that?" Josh asked, becoming curious like Aliyah and I.

"Well, his parents are not able to pick him up at this moment, and no one can watch him until his parents come," Mrs. Colswerth answered.

"Why can't any of the teachers watch him?" I asked.

"They are all in a meeting, and the meeting will take a while. None of the teachers were planning for a student to get sick before the trip. So now we have to delay the trip for an hour until the student's guardian picks him up," she answered and went to tell the bus driver.

"So, what are we supposed to do now?" Josh asked.

"I guess we just sit here and wait," I answered.

"I hate waiting. I wonder who got sick," Aliyah said.

"I was wondering the same thing," I said.

"It was probably Johnny. I didn't see him get on the bus," Josh said.

"Now that you mention it, I didn't see him get on either. He was in class though. Mrs. Colswerth called his name, and I heard him respond."

All I could hear was everyone talking loudly, probably wondering why we were not heading to the stables yet. About twenty minutes passed while everyone talked and waited.

"Hey, Sara," a voice called out to me.

I turned to see that it was Brittney. She's my friend, but not as close as I am with Aliyah and Josh. She has long dark wavy brown hair with sapphire eyes. If you don't know what a sapphire is, it's a dark-blue gem that is very pretty, so her eyes are dark blue. She usually wears blue tank-top shirts with a white light sweater. She also wears blue jeans, white sneakers, and big silver hoop earrings.

"What's going on? Why haven't we gone yet?" Brittney asked.

"Oh, well you see…" I started, but stopped when I heard the bus horn.

I turned to see that Mrs. Colswerth was starting to say something to everyone.

Suddenly, it became silent because everyone wanted to listen to Mrs. Colswerth. I knew that they all just wanted to find out why we were not going anywhere. Then the bus started to move, and everyone cheered in excitement. The bus horn blew again to make everyone silent.

"I'm sorry it took a while, but now we are on our way. So, everyone, remain seated until we stop for lunch," Mrs. Colswerth said.

Everyone started to talk again, and when I looked out the window at the school one more time, I saw Johnny with an older gentlemen walking to a car.

"So it was Johnny. I guess that must be his uncle or something because Mrs. Colswerth said his parents couldn't pick him up. It was only twenty minutes, not an hour," I said to myself, but I didn't worry about it.

"Sweet, we're finally on our way," Josh said with enthusiasm.

"Yeah, we are," I said while looking out the window.

Johnny usually wears black clothes like black shirts, black shoes, and even black jeans. He likes the gothic vibe, and he has black hair too. He has dark eyes that are even darker than Aliyah's eyes. He also has his nose and eyebrow pierced. Some of my other friends are goth too, but unfortunately, they didn't want to come and be with horses.

Johnny's usually timid and doesn't like to be in a large crowd. He and I got along well, and I think he's my friend. I consider him to be my friend, but he never smiles when we talk.

He was really looking forward to this trip. I felt bad for him, and I hoped he feels better. I wondered how he got so sick that he couldn't come on the trip with us.

"I wonder how long it's going to take until we stop for lunch," Josh said.

"How can you be hungry? We just left?" Aliyah asked.

"I never ate breakfast this morning," he answered.

"Why didn't you eat breakfast?" I asked.

"I was too busy packing," he answered.

"You mean you didn't pack the day before?" I asked.

"Yeah, that's exactly what I mean," he answered.

"Why do you pack the day before the trip? I usually pack a week before it," Aliyah said.

"I normally just pack two days before the trip," I answered.

"Okay, I guess. Oh, and I remembered to bring my song book," Aliyah said.

"That's great. Now we can sing all we want during the trip," I said.

Aliyah also writes songs, and we sing them all the time when we have the time to do it. They are really good songs, and they even express her feelings. The class usually loves to hear us sing, so we always make sure we do our best when we sing.

2

On the way to lunch during the trip, I told Aliyah and Josh that Johnny was the student who got sick. I also daydreamed most of the way there. I dream about a lot of different stuff, but this time I daydreamed about what Johnny did that got him sick. I was worried about him.

Suddenly, I felt a tap on my shoulder. When I turned to look, it was Aliyah.

"What's wrong, Sara? You haven't talked since we left," Aliyah said.

"Oh, I've just been thinking," I answered.

"Thinking about what, Sara?" Josh asked, looking at me.

"I was thinking about Johnny," I answered.

"What about him?" Aliyah asked.

"I was wondering who picked him up so early. I mean, didn't Mrs. Colswerth say that it would take an hour before someone picked him up?" I asked.

I just couldn't stop thinking about it even though I probably won't be able to find out, but I just had a strange feeling about it.

"Yeah, I was wondering the same thing," Josh said.

"Yeah, right! All you talked about was food, but you said nothing about Johnny," Aliyah said, nudging him in the arm.

I was a bit envious of Aliyah because every time I tried to talk casually with Josh and play-slap his arm, I get nervous and clam up, which is why I try to keep Aliyah next to me when I talk to him.

"Okay, so I lied. I guess I never thought about it. I thought it was an hour," Josh admitted.

"It was only twenty minutes," I said, not looking him in the eyes.

"How could I keep track of time?" Josh asked.

Josh complains a lot when there is nothing to do, so he just makes up lots of different things to talk about. Sometimes, when he was really bored, he would just say whatever popped in his mind, and we would talk about it. For example, we once had a long discussion on if cats could see ghosts or not. That topic lasted two whole days, and we still never finished it.

"Aliyah, can I see your song book for a moment?" I asked.

"Yeah, sure," Aliyah answered and handed me her song book.

I started to get a little tired because I woke up early. Usually when I keep myself preoccupied, I'm able to stay awake. So I looked at her song book to see all the different songs she wrote.

There are love songs, dream songs, make-up-and break-up songs, songs that made you cry, songs that talked about feelings—I could keep going on and on, but one song caught my eye.

It was a dream song that sounded really beautiful, so I started humming it. When I did, Aliyah started to hum with me. Then we started to sing:

> Every night when I fall asleep
> All I think about is what I can be
> Or what I can do
> And prove the world I'm somebody
> I dream that one day
> I can be part famous
> Someone who can be well known.

Suddenly everyone became silent because they always loved to hear us sing. We continued to sing, but for this part I sang alone:

> At a land full of mysteries
> Or a land full of fantasies
> Every day I wish upon a star
> Wondering when that day comes
> Or when is it my turn
> But all I can do is dream…

Then it was Aliyah's turn to sing the next part:

> Someday the person I dream of will come
> I believe it with all my heart
> Until the one day comes
> All I do is sit and dream, hoping that
> Someday it will happen
> I pray and hope and dream again.

There was a part we both sang. It was "Ooohhh…" and then I started to notice that everyone was staring at us including Mrs. Colswerth. Of course, Josh was watching us too, so I sang a little louder for everyone to hear:

> At a land full of mysteries
> Or a land full of fantasies
> Every day I wish upon a star
> Wondering when that day comes
> Or when is it my turn
> But all I can do is dream…

It was so nice and peaceful that some girls were humming and some boys were making a beat. That started to make everyone want to join in, and Aliyah started to sing louder than ever:

> In every dream there's a happily ever after
> But I wonder when my day will come
> I'm not gonna rush it.

There was a part that I sang in it, and Aliyah sang the rest of the part. This is the part I sang:

> I'mma let it come on its own…

And Aliyah sang the rest:

> So I dream and dream
> And it feels *so* real I pray someday
> And dream that I can be…

Then we sang the rest of the song together in perfect harmony while all the girls, even Mrs. Colswerth, hummed along, and all the boys made a slow beat including Josh. So we sang:

> At a land full of mysteries
> Or a land full of fantasies
> Every day I wish upon a star
> Wondering when that day comes
> Or when is it my turn
> But all I can do is dream…

Then we sang even louder and more in harmony than ever:

> At a land full of mysteries
> Or a land full of fantasies
> Every day I wish upon a star
> Wondering when that day comes
> Or when is it my turn
> But all I can do is dream…

Aliyah and I slowed down, and everyone stopped so they could listen:

> Every night when I go to sleep…

I sang the rest of the song, and Aliyah had *yeh*s at the end, so I sang this part:

> I…dream…

I held the dream, and Aliyah did:

Yeh, yeh, yeh, yeh…

Then we both took a deep breath at the end, and everyone cheered for us, clapping their hands as the bus pulled to a stop.
The bus driver yelled over everyone's cheering, "We're here!"
Everyone cheered some more and started heading off the bus.

3

After everyone ate lunch, we got back on the bus. I was tired, so I told Aliyah and Josh that I was going to sleep and close my eyes. At first, I was resting, listening to everyone talk. As the bus's gentle movement rocked me to sleep, I started to dream of what the Crest Hill Stables was going to be like.

Suddenly the scene in my head changed from a red barn to a glowing bright light, and the shadow of a woman appeared. She was standing in front of the stables. I couldn't see what she looked like because of the bright light around her, but she had a very gentle-sounding voice that said to me, "Look for Silver Dash. Help him. He needs someone to guide him."

"Who is Silver Dash?" I asked, sounding like I was talking from very far away.

"Please help him. He needs to run," the voice said in reply.

Then she disappeared, and I woke up. I jerked up and saw the stables out the window. I couldn't remember what the woman looked like. She was too foggy to see, but I could remember the voice—that sweet, gentle-sounding voice. I would never forget that. Someone tapped me on the shoulder, and I turned to see that it was Aliyah.

"Can you see the Crest Hill Stables, Sara?" Aliyah asked.

"Yeah, I see it, and it's beautiful," I answered.

"It's huge," Josh said.

"I know. How big do you think it is?" Aliyah asked.

"I don't know. What are you asking me for?" Josh asked.

I couldn't concentrate. All I could think about was who that woman in my dream was. *Who is Silver Dash? Is he at the stables? Is he a person? I hope that my questions will be answered when we arrive.*

When we got closer to the stables, Mrs. Colswerth stood up at the front of the bus. "Everyone, listen up," Mrs. Colswerth shouted.

Everyone was too excited to stop talking, so Mrs. Colswerth had to yell: "Students!"

No one listened, so Aliyah stood up and yelled, "*Quiet!*"

Aliyah was so loud I had to cover my ears, but it worked, and everyone stopped talking.

"Thank you, Aliyah," Mrs. Colswerth said. I think she had to cover her ears too.

The bus stopped, and I realized we were at the entrance to the Crest Hill Stables.

"We are at the stables, so, everyone, grab your trash or anything else that you brought onto the bus with you. We don't want to leave any mess on the bus," Mrs. Colswerth emphasized.

Everyone started to pick up any trash they found on the floor. I helped Aliyah because I didn't have anything with me. Aliyah was clean and tidy, so I didn't need to help all that much.

Josh, on the other hand, needed most of the help. He's so dirty and unorganized that there was too much trash for him to handle, so Aliyah and I helped him and got off the bus once we were done.

All three of us stood there in awe. Other students were getting off the bus and stared with us at the amazing sight. The smell of horse hair, hay barrels, and manure was strong. The Crest Hill Stables was bigger than any of us thought it would be.

The stable was three floors, was as long as about three buses, and was made of dull dark-red bricks with a black roof and a dull red chimney. The chimney probably got that color from all the rain, which paled the color a bit from the dark red-brick of the main building. There was a paddock for the horses to graze in to the left of the stables though parts of the fence were missing or were broken.

A paddock is an area where horses can be outside but are fenced in so they can't run away. I could see a few chestnut-colored horses in there and a pure-black horse. That black horse was alone while the chestnut horses grazed in the corner, which seemed odd.

That black horse had the whole field, and it looked like the chestnut horses were afraid of him. I used to ride horses when I was young and still do now and again with Aliyah at a stable closer to home. I could always feel what they were thinking, which is why I love horses so much.

They are free and majestic looking while having strong emotions. They can always feel what you are feeling even before you knew what it was you were feeling. They are amazing creatures who love to be in herds.

To the right of the stables, I could see the racetrack. It's a huge racetrack with a few horses and their riders running it, getting ready for the big race coming up at the end of the week.

A racetrack is this big oval-shaped track the horses run on to race. There is a special kind of sand on the track so the horses will not hurt themselves while they run. When racehorses run, they can run up to forty miles per hour, so they need cushion for any accidents that might happen during a race. If the horse trips and falls, the rider and horse won't get hurt as badly when they fall if there wasn't any sand to protect them. The sand also gives traction for the horses to run on and takes care of their hooves while they run.

This track was a little different as it was smaller than a normal racetrack can be. This made the race all that more exciting since the horse and rider—jockey is the professional term for a rider in a race—had to run three laps of the track in order to win.

There was going to be a huge competition on Saturday to see which horse is the fastest in the stable. We were going to watch it and choose which horse we think will win the championship. There would also be small races to see which horses will be picked for the championship in a group. It's going to be a lot of fun. I always wished I could be in a race, and I always wanted to see how it would feel to be on a racetrack. Saturday night, after the championship race, we would be able to ride horses on the track. What a perfect way to end the school year.

A tall muscular man with pale skin and a brown-bearded face came to greet us. He had short ruffled brown hair and brown eyes like his hair. He wore a brown shirt with gray riding pants and tall black riding boots. Mrs. Colswerth went to meet him. They talked for a few seconds, and then the man came toward us.

"My name is Johnson, but everyone calls me Mr. Johnson here. I am the owner of the Crest Hill Stables, and I thank you all for coming to see the race. It is nice to see all of you, and I hope you all have a good time here," he said with a voice deep and strong.

Then he saw me and stared very hard at me for several long moments. His eyes widened, and I felt a little nervous as he did because he had a surprised—almost sad—look on his face. I don't remember meeting him, but he was acting like he had seen me before.

Mrs. Colswerth broke his stare when she said, "All right, everyone, let's go in now."

Everyone started to head toward the stables, but I waited because Aliyah wanted to take a picture of the stables. Mr. Johnson continued to stare at me a little longer before he left with the students.

I kept watching him until Aliyah broke my concentration when she said, "Sara, come on. I want to see what it's like on the inside."

"Yeah, come on, slowpoke," Josh yelled a little farther away, reaching the stables before us.

Aliyah and Josh were ahead of me, going inside. I started following them when I saw Johnny with that same old guy who picked him up at school either.

He saw me and started to run toward me. When I looked for Aliyah and Josh, they were already inside with everyone else. When I turned, Johnny was there.

"Johnny? What are you doing here?" I asked.

"My grandpa works here," he answered, looking surprisingly healthy even though he was supposed to be sick.

"But I thought you had gotten sick and couldn't come?" I asked.

"Well, it's a long story. The short part is that I lied about being sick and called my uncle to pick me up," he answered.

"Why did you lie?" I asked with confusion.

"I don't want to talk about it. Sorry," he answered, rubbing the back of his head.

"Then why are you here?" I asked since he didn't seem willing to tell me about why he lied, so I changed the subject.

"Since my parents couldn't pick me up because they're out of town, my uncle had to. He was on his way here and near the school, so I asked him to pick me up," Johnny answered.

"So your uncle works here?" I asked.

"Yep," Johnny said with a nod.

An old man, who was the person I saw pick up Johnny at school, with grayish-white hair, wearing an old wrinkled white shirt with blue pants and small glasses that looked like reading glasses came out to greet us. He had grayish eyes, but they looked young like he was still full of life.

He called out to Johnny, "Hey, Johnny!" He had a deep, wrinkled old voice. It sounded happy though. Johnny and I looked at him.

"That's my uncle. Uncle Ben is what everyone calls him," Johnny answered.

His uncle kept walking toward us. When he got closer, he stopped and stared at me. He had the same surprised look Mr. Johnson had when he first saw me too. Johnny looked confused, looking at his uncle and me. I just couldn't stop staring back at Johnny's uncle. I got the same feeling when Mr. Johnson stared. I felt nervous—like something was wrong.

Finally, Johnny broke the staring contest between his uncle and me. "Uncle Ben, this is my friend Sara."

"I see," Johnny's uncle replied.

"It's nice to meet you, sir," I said, still feeling a bit nervous but trying to be polite.

Johnny's uncle just kept staring, not taking his eyes off me for one second.

"Uncle Ben? What's wrong?" Johnny asked.

Finally, Johnny's uncle stopped staring. He looked over to Johnny. "I'm sorry—nothing is wrong. I wanted to see who your friend was."

Then he looked over to me. This time, he looked confused.

"My name is Ben Ross. As you know, I'm Johnny's uncle. You may call me Uncle Ben if you wish. Everyone else does." Uncle Ben chuckled. Then he asked me with hesitation, "Are you, by any chance, related to Lucile Cameron?"

"No, I'm not. I don't even know who that is. If you don't mind me asking, Uncle Ben, why do you think I'm related to her?" I asked since I didn't know her.

"Well, you look exactly like her. You could be her twin, but she died last year, so I thought I was looking at her ghost," Uncle Ben answered.

That's creepy! I thought to myself. Suddenly the dream I had popped into my mind. That moment changed my life forever.

4

"Oh, she died? How did she die? Did she work here?" I asked. Now I was confused. *How could I look like someone I don't even know?*

"She used to be a jockey here. She was the reigning champion here until she got in a bad accident. She and her horse got seriously injured. Her horse recovered, but sadly she didn't. She died shortly after the accident happened, and it devastated the stables," Uncle Ben answered.

"That's awful. I'm so sorry," I said in reply.

"Hey, Sara," someone called out.

When we turned toward the stable, it was Aliyah calling me. She was waving to me to come over inside.

"Oh, is that your friend? Let's not keep her waiting," Uncle Ben said.

When I looked back, I saw that Johnny disappeared. I guess he didn't want anyone else to know he's here. Uncle Ben started walking, and I followed.

"Hello, young lady. My name is Ben Ross, but you may call me Uncle Ben," Uncle Ben said to Aliyah.

"Hi, I'm Aliyah. Sara, where did you go? I've been looking all over for you," Aliyah said.

"Sorry, Aliyah. I was talking to Uncle Ben here. He's actually Johnny's uncle," I answered.

"Really? Well, it's nice to meet you, Uncle Ben," Aliyah said, shaking Uncle Ben's hand. Then she grabbed mine, and I could tell she was confused. I think she wanted to talk about it more but also wanted to see the horses as much as I do.

"Come on, Sara. Mr. Johnson is going to show us all the horses," Aliyah said.

Then she pulled me in the direction of where the horses are. She took my luggage and put it with the rest of the luggage everyone put in the corner of the stables.

It looked beautiful on the inside. The interior was made of chestnut wood. There were saddles and bridles hanging up on the wall with names over them. Some said WILD NIGHT, SHINING STAR, SILVER DASH…

Then I stopped. I didn't realize that I also stopped Aliyah with me since we were still holding hands. I stared at that name, and I remembered that was the same name from my dream the beautifully voiced woman had said I needed to help. The saddle and bridle looked dirty and unused, almost as if the owner never cleaned it or…

I stopped to think.

If Silver Dash is a horse, then who was the lady in my dream, and why does she want me to help him?

If I was right, which horse is Silver Dash?

"What's wrong, Sara?" Aliyah said, breaking my concentration. I looked at her, and she looked worried.

"Are you okay? I've been saying your name for a while. Were you daydreaming again?" Aliyah asked.

"Sorry, I was thinking of something. I didn't mean to scare you," I answered.

"Well, come on. We are going to miss seeing the horses," Aliyah said, dragging me further into the enormous stables.

Then we met up with everyone else. I could hear Mr. Johnson talking while everyone looked around at the horses. I was not paying attention one bit though; I didn't hear anything that Mr. Johnson said. My mind was still whirling in my head. Aliyah let go of my hand when we saw the first horse.

All the horses were in stalls that had a lot of room. There was hay on the floor of the stalls, two blue buckets of water inside each of the entrances to the stalls. You could see the bits of hay floating all over inside the stables with a strong smell of alfalfa. There was alfalfa in the back corner of the stalls for the horses to eat. Alfalfa is a type of hay that is good for horses to eat. There was also a red bucket with horse feed, usually a type of grain, in it next to the buckets of water.

Horse feed looks a little like birdseed but has nutrients for the horses. The stalls were lined up on both sides of the walls—ten stalls on each side—making a total of twenty horses in the stables.

The first horse I saw was a beautiful chestnut with a white snip on its nose. A snip is a white line only on a horse's nose. He had a darker-colored mane and tail. The name on the stall said CHESTNUT BARLEY, which sounded like an appropriate name to me.

I looked over to the next stall and saw the name written as SHINING STAR—that was the name before SILVER DASH, with the dirty saddle and bridle. I looked at Shining Star, and he was gorgeous. He had a light-color chestnut coat with a beautiful white star on his forehead. It was in the shape of a perfect star, which was probably how he got the name. His mane and tail were a little darker than his coat.

Before I went to the next stall, I heard a loud thud. I looked over and saw a horse—a beautiful silver horse. A few men were trying to take the horse out of his stall, but he didn't want to go out. The men got some control of the horse and brought him out of the stall. The beautiful horse tried hard to fight back though.

The horse had a silver-gray coat. His mane and tail started out gray and changed to silver near the bottom. He had a dark-gray pastern on his left hind leg. A pastern is a different color shade of hair on the horse's leg that is right above the hoof.

The horse kept rearing up while the men tried to hold him down with ropes. The poor horse kept whinnying, which broke my heart. He was hurting though I didn't know *how* I knew that.

"That's Silver Dash, Lucile's horse," Uncle Ben said, standing next to me.

I didn't notice him. I also didn't notice that I was in front of everyone while they watched the men hold the horse down. I noticed Mr. Johnson walking in front of me, heading toward the horse.

"Wait, that's Lucile's horse?" I asked Uncle Ben.

I was right about Silver Dash being a horse. Now I knew who Silver Dash was. I just didn't know who that lady in my dream was or how I could help her now that I found Silver Dash.

"Stop, men! Let the horse be," Mr. Johnson yelled in a deep voice to the men holding Silver Dash.

"But, sir…" one of the men started to say when one of the ropes snapped, releasing the hold on Silver Dash.

Silver Dash reared up, and the men lost hold of the ropes. Silver Dash turned and started to canter toward Mr. Johnson.

Then in that one moment, Silver Dash and I saw each other for the first time, our eyes staying locked on each other. Silver Dash slowed to a stop. We stared at each other for a long time, and my heart soared with a knowledge that we were meant to help each other. Mr. Johnson, the men who held onto Silver Dash, Uncle Ben, and all of my classmates, including Mrs. Colswerth, just stared at us, waiting for something—what, I don't know.

Silver Dash started to walk toward me. No one moved or stopped him. I couldn't move either. I was so mesmerized by him that I didn't want to move at all.

Silver Dash stopped right in front of me, staring into my eyes. I stared into his beautiful dark sea-blue eyes. I raised my hand in front of his nose, and he put his nose right into my hand so I can pet him. I smiled, feeling at peace, and pet his forehead with my other hand.

Everyone was stunned into silence for several minutes.

"Just as I thought," Uncle Ben said, smiling with tears in his eyes.

Mr. Johnson smiled at Uncle Ben and then at me with a knowing look I didn't understand. I didn't have a care in the world at that moment. I just wanted to keep looking at Silver Dash and having this feeling in my heart that we were meant to meet.

5

After Mr. Johnson and Uncle Ben put Silver Dash back in his stall, they said they wanted to show me something. The rest of the class continued with the tour except Aliyah and Josh. They asked if they could come.

After a few minutes of convincing, Mr. Johnson and Uncle Ben said they could come. Aliyah, Josh, and I followed Mr. Johnson and Uncle Ben to the second floor.

The second floor has the same chestnut wood interior, but instead of stalls, saddles, and bridles, there are closets. Each jockey has his or her own closet full of brushes, cleaning supplies, and trophies.

"Why are we here?" Aliyah asked.

No one answered until we stopped at a certain closet with a bunch of white calla lilies in front of it. These flowers are usually found in funerals for the dead as well as representing rebirth for those who believe in a life after death.

"We are here because of this…" Mr. Johnson said, opening the door.

Aliyah, Josh, and I gasped. There were trophies and metals on every countertop with pictures of Silver Dash all over the walls. In the back was a table with the biggest trophy I had ever seen. There was a picture of a woman all around the trophy, with a few pictures of Silver Dash next to her, holding the trophies.

Uncle Ben picked up a picture of the woman and handed it to me, which I stared at with an open mouth. "That is Lucile." Uncle Ben said.

Aliyah and Josh looked at it and gasped again in total shock.

"Wow, Sara. That woman looks just like you," Aliyah said—and she's right. Lucile had the same face, hair, and eye color as me. We truly look like we could be twins.

"You could be twins," Josh said as if hearing my own thoughts.

"That is why I said I was seeing a ghost of Lucile," Uncle Ben said soberly.

"I'm sorry I stared at you, but now you know why, Sara," Mr. Johnson said, his usual deep voice quiet and sad.

Uncle Ben picked up another picture from the table and handed it to me, saying, "That's when Lucile won the Championship Cup two years ago."

The picture had Lucile in a white-with-black-lining riding uniform with a big trophy, standing next to Silver Dash. The trophy in the picture was the same trophy on the table.

I looked over to the trophy, and it was pure gold that was in a shape of a cup with a large base supporting it. On the cup was an outline of a racing horse and a jockey. The horse had dash marks behind it to show that it was the fastest horse in the race. Near the bottom was black plate with writing on it with Lucile's name and the date of when she won the Championship Cup. When I looked down at the bottom of the closet, there were four other trophies just like it.

"She got her dream of winning the Championship Cup and kept winning for five years straight. She still rode Silver Dash until last year, when she died," Uncle Ben said with nostalgia.

"Lucile wanted to ride Silver Dash on the racetrack one night. What she didn't know was that part of the sand had a ditch in it, probably from not being paved like it should have been or the terrible storm the day before or from a rodent that occasionally digs—we don't know for sure," Mr. Johnson continued as they both told the story.

"She was only going at a canter, but she didn't see the ditch until it was too late. It had started to rain, and the wind picked up. Silver Dash fell in and hurt his leg real bad. Lucile fell off Silver Dash, but he started to kick and buck," Uncle Ben said.

"Lucile broke her wrist when she fell. She tried to get Silver Dash to calm down, but his leg was stuck in the ditch. The ditch was too deep, and the rain only made his front leg sink in more. She tried to pull his leg out, but it hurt his leg so much that he kicked her in the ribs," Mr. Johnson continued.

"Lucile had about two broken ribs after Silver Dash kicked her. She would not stop though. She tried again to get his leg free, and it worked. However, when Silver Dash tried to stand, he fell on Lucile," Uncle Ben led on.

"Silver Dash couldn't get up because he was lying on the side of his bad leg. This made Lucile's injuries even worse. When we got there after hearing all the noise, it was too late. Lucile was dying of massive internal bleeding, and she died shortly after getting to the hospital," Mr. Johnson said.

"Silver Dash recovered after two months, but he still waited for her to return. He did not mean to kill her, but his spirit was broken, and he never recovered mentally from that. He has not been ridden in over a year, and he never lets anyone else ride him. He always fights us when we try to take him out of his stall to get exercise," Uncle Ben said, finishing the story.

"Silver Dash only ever let Lucile ride him. No one else has ever ridden him. He has a missing part of his heart that has been ripped away for so long. Now that he saw you, Sara, he believes you are Lucile come back," Mr. Johnson said.

Aliyah, Josh, and I all said at the same time, "What?"

"Silver Dash believes that Lucile has come back for him. If I am correct about his thoughts, he might let you ride him, Sara," Uncle Ben said. He had happiness in his voice that was hopeful.

"So, you're saying that only Sara can ride Silver Dash? Are you sure that's a good idea?" Josh asked nervously.

"That's exactly what I'm saying," Uncle Ben answered and then stared into my eyes with a strong look. "If you don't try, Silver Dash will fade away. He has been fading, losing weight, and not running for a whole year. That's not healthy for a horse, and if that continues, he will eventually die of a broken heart."

I put the pictures back on the table in the closet. I was still mesmerized by the story Mr. Johnson and Uncle Ben told us. I started to think of what that woman in my dream told me: "Help Silver Dash… He needs to run…"

I started to think that maybe I should try it. *I should at least try to help him if I can, right?*

"I'll do it," I said, feeling those words hit me straight in the heart. Those words felt right to me. *This feels right to me even though I don't know why that is.*

"You will? That will be wonderful. Silver Dash can run again," Uncle Ben said happily.

"Now hold on there. First we need to see if Silver Dash will truly let Sara ride him before we jump to conclusions. We also have to see how Sara does while riding. You can ride, can't you?" Mr. Johnson said loudly, his strong voice coming back, and seemed to have some hope lining his features.

"Yes, I can ride. Aliyah and I take riding lessons back home," I answered.

"Let's do it," Aliyah and Josh said at the same time. Then they looked at each other, surprised, and I giggled.

We all left the closet area and headed toward the stairs. Suddenly Johnny came running up the stairs, stopping in front of his uncle.

"Uncle, there's…" Then he stopped, seeing all of us there. Aliyah and Josh looked surprised.

"Johnny, what are you doing here? I thought you went home," Aliyah asked.

"That's a long story. You see…" Johnny started to say until Uncle Ben stepped in, interrupting him.

"Answer that question later, Johnny. What is wrong?" Uncle Ben asked with concern in his voice.

"It's bad—you have to come down right away," Johnny answered, turning and running down the stairs. We all followed Johnny down the stairs and heard screaming.

When we got to the first floor, a ferocious big pure-black horse with a black mane and tail was bucking and jumping. His whinnies had anger in them as it took more men to try and hold him down than Silver Dash did.

"That's Wild Night," Mr. Johnson said in a low gruff voice.

I remembered that name from the name over the saddle and bridle we saw earlier. The horse looked like the same horse from the paddock outside where he took over most of the grass area while the other horses stood far away from him while he ate. The saddle and bridle were also black.

"He's going nuts," Josh said.

"Yeah, he's worse than Silver Dash," Aliyah agreed.

Johnny stayed back so no one else could see him. Mr. Johnson and Uncle Ben moved toward Wild Night. They also grabbed ropes to try and calm Wild Night down.

Then a tall man with a broom came in. He was wearing dirty dark-colored green clothes, black riding boots, and was holding a black hat. He had dark-brown hair and brown eyes that looked similar to Wild Night's. He went up to the rampaged horse, and when Wild Night saw him, he stopped completely. The man went up to pet Wild Night while everyone stared.

Then he glared at me, grabbing the ropes and taking Wild Night into his stall. All the other men were breathing deeply from that excitement including Mr. Johnson and Uncle Ben. Once the man was done taking care of Wild Night, he looked at me one more time and left with a frown. Mr. Johnson and Uncle Ben came back over to us.

"Who was that?" I asked, feeling like I need to know who that man was. I was a little suspicious of him.

"That was Buck. He cleans the stalls for the horses. For some reason, Wild Night only lets him do what he just did—pets him, feeds him, takes him out—but no one else can. We can't seem to control that horse anymore, and we are going to let him retire after this year," Mr. Johnson answered.

"If the stables is still up and running," Uncle Ben mumbled under his breath.

What does that mean? Are the rumors about the stables closing true?

Everyone relaxed, and the class went upstairs to see the closets while our group stayed downstairs.

"Well, how about we try what we were going to do earlier? Sara, are you ready?" Uncle Ben asked.

"Yes, I'm ready," I answered, my heart beating wildly in my chest with excitement. When I turned around, Johnny was gone.

"Hey, where's Johnny?" Aliyah asked my question for me, noticing that Johnny was missing too.

"He probably went to clean the attic—that's his job here. The attic holds all of our storage materials there like the hay barrels and other small equipment," Uncle Ben answered.

"Why is he here anyway? I thought he went back home," Josh asked.

"I thought so too," Aliyah agreed.

"I will tell you two later. For now, let us worry about the task at hand," Uncle Ben answered, gesturing toward Silver Dash's stall.

He knew why Johnny lied, so it seemed like he might tell us later, depending on how everything went.

We walked toward Silver Dash's stall. When we got there, Silver Dash was eating alfalfa as though nothing had happened. All the other horses were in the backs of their stalls, looking frightened. Silver Dash, on the other hand, looked as if he just didn't care.

"He's eating," Uncle Ben said to Mr. Johnson excitedly. They both looked relieved since Silver Dash apparently had not been eating all that much.

"Silver Dash," I said in a nice, sweet voice.

He jerked his head up and whinnied at me. He trotted over to me as close as he could get. He was happy to see me and I put my hand up to his nose like I did the first time and he put his nose in my hand again to pet him.

Every part of my soul felt this was right to have us together like this—almost like fate knew we needed each other to feel whole.

"He only let Lucile pet and tack him, so let's see if he will let you tack him instead," Mr. Johnson said.

Mr. Johnson got Silver Dash's saddle and bridle while Uncle Ben got grooming supplies from Lucile's closet.

When they got back, Mr. Johnson said, "Only you can take Silver Dash out of his stall, Sara."

I opened the stall door, but Silver Dash stood still. He watched me as I took a lead line and hooked it up to his halter. He didn't move until I was set and started walking out of the stall with me. He followed me without a jerk or a kick; he was calm and didn't feel nervous. Aliyah and Josh were surprised to see that Silver Dash didn't fight. Mr. Johnson and Uncle Ben looked pleased to see that their assumption was correct.

When I stopped, Silver Dash stopped as well without me having to pull on the rope. He was quick to respond to my movements and seemed to understand what I wanted to do.

"Lucile and Silver Dash always had a strong connection. You may be able to have a similar connection as well with him. To be safe, though, keep the lead line on him, but you may be able to work with him without the lead line once the both of you have a strong connection together," Uncle Ben said.

"What do you mean?" I asked, confused.

"I mean you do not have to hold the lead line. Silver Dash will only listen to what you tell him to do," Uncle Ben answered.

"Lucile never used a lead line. Silver Dash always listened to her, and they were always able to understand each other to the point that they each knew what the other wanted," Mr. Johnson added.

"First, see if Silver Dash will work with you by having him stay still while you brush him down," Uncle Ben suggested.

I started to use a curry comb—a type of comb in the shape of a circle you use to loosen the underside of a horse's hair—on Silver Dash's side and slowly let go of the lead line. I felt Silver Dash relax under the comb while I brushed him, and he stayed perfectly still while I brushed his body, mane and tail, and picked the undersides of his hooves.

I walked back and forth all around Silver Dash, always having a hand on him without ever touching the lead line, and he just watched me with glee in his beautiful blue eyes.

"Yes, and now that we know Silver Dash will work with you, let's see if you can ride him," Mr. Johnson said after I was done brushing Silver Dash.

Mr. Johnson handed me a jockey uniform that was mostly white with black lining with the number one on the back of the jacket, a white helmet, black knee-high riding boots, and a crop. This uniform looked similar to the one Lucile wore, but I didn't ask if it was the same one.

Jockeys wear a specific uniform for races, all similar styles to riding pant leathers and jackets which usually have different colors to know who is riding in a race. The knee-high boots protect the shins as well as the horse's belly and are almost always black. A crop is a short stick with a wide leather strap at the end that jockeys use to lightly smack the horse's rear to have them run faster. I, however, know that I don't need to use the crop on Silver Dash. Usually the blankets underneath the saddles on the horse have a similar color to the one the jockey wears with numbers on them.

I found a changing room and got myself ready. When I came out, Silver Dash's tack gear was set out for me to tack him. I noticed that the blanket for Silver Dash was white with black number one on it.

I tacked Silver Dash up with a bridle and saddle and followed Mr. Johnson to the racetrack. Silver Dash followed me without me needing to lead him with the rains. Aliyah, Josh, and Uncle Ben followed behind us. When we got to the racetrack, Silver Dash looked alert, looking on the ground to make sure nothing was there.

"We fixed the ditch and checked the whole racetrack after the accident, so everything is safe now to ride," Mr. Johnson said after noticing Silver Dash's reaction.

"However, Silver Dash does not seem to be relaxed. How about letting him see the racetrack for himself, Sara?" Uncle Ben insisted.

"Silver Dash…" I said, and he looked at me.

I continued, "Go check the racetrack for yourself—if that will make you feel better."

He snorted and nodded while trotting off. Silver Dash went to a certain part of the racetrack, and I started to wonder why.

"That is amazing. He still remembers," Uncle Ben said in astonishment.

"What? What does he remember?" Aliyah asked anxiously, watching from behind the fence.

"He remembers the spot where Lucile died. Even after a year, he never forgot," Mr. Johnson answered.

Silver Dash sniffed the sand everywhere near that spot. When he was satisfied, he trotted back to me. He stopped right in front of me as if to say that the area is safe.

"Thank you, Silver Dash," I said, gently petting him.

"Now it is time, Sara. Ride Silver Dash," Uncle Ben insisted, standing next to me, cupping his hands for me to mount.

"Are you ready to run, Silver Dash?" I asked, and he snorted as if to say, "I was born ready."

I mounted Silver Dash by putting my foot in Uncle Ben's hands and settling on the saddle once I had my feet in the stirrups. Once I sat on Silver Dash, his whole demeanor changed. He was still and straight, waiting for me to be ready, his muscles twitching in excitement I can feel radiating off him. His ears flickered back and forth, and his breathing became steadier.

When I'm set, Mr. Johnson said, "Be careful! He's fast, and once you start going, you have to be diligent. Tell him what to do, and he'll listen."

Everyone backed away, and I can feel Silver Dash trying to hold back all his excitement until I told him to go. I stared at the racetrack to see how long it went. The smell of dirt and grass became stronger to me while the wind lightly breezed by. I had to take off my glasses since they could fall off and break. Luckily, I remembered to bring my contacts, so I hoped that the dirt didn't get into my eyes.

I got into my two-point position—that's when your butt is off the horse's back and you bend toward the horse's neck. The heels of my feet were down in the stirrups, and my hands held onto the reins with my crop in my right hand.

I pushed my hands forward to give Silver Dash room to move his head while he ran. I squeezed my thighs, not my shins, to hold on since I was using my feet and thighs to hold me up in my two-point position.

I whispered into Silver Dash's ear, "Silver Dash, *go!*"

6

Silver Dash whinnied and reared up in excitement. I held on as hard as I could so I wouldn't fall off. Then he suddenly went into a gallop, soaring across the racetrack with his ears pinned back against his head. The wind was flying across my face, and everything around me was a blur of motion. Silver Dash was running so fast it felt like we were flying in the sky like a bird. I closed my eyes for a brief moment to feel the rush of running like the wind, trusting Silver Dash to take care of me.

I knew that this was a dangerous thing to do while riding a horse, since I could easily get hurt or the horse could trip without being guided, but I knew deep down that I could trust Silver Dash completely. Besides, it only took a moment to calm my racing heart and steady my adrenaline rush that overpowered me as we ran.

My body shook back and forth in a steady rhythm; I was in sync with Silver Dash's stride. Stride is the type of motion a horse is moving while running. When I opened my eyes, I realized that I was passing everyone for the second time. It wasn't that long that we had started running, yet Silver Dash didn't seem to know the meaning of slow.

When I passed, somehow things slowed a little for me to see enough that Aliyah and Josh were smiling in awe, and Uncle Ben and Mr. Johnson were keeping time with a stopwatch in both of their hands. They looked like they were impressed with the time. Silver Dash just kept running! I thought he would get tired, but he kept the same pace for a while.

Then I heard that same beautiful voice call out, "Let him run."
Lucile! She has to be the woman in my dreams.

Silver Dash was so happy that I listened to the voice and let him run for as long as he wanted to. I lost count on how many laps we did, but near maybe the third or fourth lap, Silver Dash started to slow down.

I went to his ear and said, "Silver Dash, you can stop."

He stopped when we were near everyone. Silver Dash and I were breathing hard; we both lost our breaths in the run. Aliyah and Josh came running up to us while Uncle Ben and Mr. Johnson were looking at each other's stopwatches.

"That was amazing!" Aliyah said while I was dismounting Silver Dash by taking both my feet out of the stirrups and swinging my right foot over the saddle to slide off Silver Dash's left side.

"I've never seen a horse run that fast before," Josh said.

"How did it feel?" Aliyah asked.

"It felt like I was flying over the track," I answered, breathless.

Silver Dash came up to me, and I put my hand up to his nose. He put his nose in my hand like always, and I pet his forehead with my other hand. Aliyah and Josh were petting Silver Dash's neck while Uncle Ben and Mr. Johnson came over to us.

"I told you he was fast," Mr. Johnson said, smiling.

"Man, is he ever," Uncle Ben said, standing next to Mr. Johnson.

"He was itching to run for so long he let it all out to actually run six laps without stopping," Uncle Ben said.

"Six laps? I thought it was only three or four," I said, surprised, my voice going up in pitch.

"It was six laps all right. Both Johnson and I counted. What great timing Silver Dash did," Uncle Ben assured me.

"Yes, it was good timing for how long he hasn't run in a while," Mr. Johnson said.

"I'm just glad he was finally able to run again," Uncle Ben said happily.

"I believe that running in the race on Friday will help him more," Mr. Johnson said suddenly.

"Are you actually thinking of—" Uncle Ben started until Mr. Johnson cut him off.

"I believe it is high time for Silver Dash to run in a race again. However, we would need a team," Mr. Johnson said.

"What do you mean by a team?" Aliyah asked.

"The rule for the Championship Race on Friday is that there must be a team of three for each race. There are three races that day in which each teammate must be in third place or higher to get into the finals. Each teammate must participate in one race for the whole team to win. The last race will have the fastest horses running it to win," Mr. Johnson said.

"If Sara gets a team and each one rides in a race to get into the finals, then Sara can ride Silver Dash in the last race?" Josh asked.

"That's correct," Uncle Ben answered.

Aliyah and Josh looked at each other, smiled, and said at the same time, "We'll do it!"

I smiled back at them while Mr. Johnson and Uncle Ben looked at each other in surprise. "Can they be my team?" I asked anxiously.

"Can they ride?" Uncle Ben asked.

"Aliyah can, and even though Josh is a little harsh, he's ridden a few times and knows what to do," I answered.

Aliyah was happy, but Josh had a mad face which made me giggle when I looked at him. I didn't mean to make him feel upset about not having as much experience as Aliyah and I, but I had to be honest.

"I would like to see them ride first, but if you trust them that much, then they can be your team," Mr. Johnson said.

"Yes! I can't wait to ride," Aliyah yelled.

"Me either. This is going to be so much fun," Josh agreed.

"First we'll need to find horses for you two to ride. It seems like we might have a winning team on our hands to save the stables, Johnson," Uncle Ben said, slapping Mr. Johnson on the back.

"What do you mean?" I asked suspiciously.

"You probably heard about it on the news, but we've been in a bit of a financial problem lately. The news didn't say why, but it was because of all the medical and veterinary fees as well as the loan on the stables that we are not sure if we are able to keep the stables running next year," Uncle Ben answered.

"Why are you explaining that to them when this should not be their concern?" Mr. Johnson sounded annoyed.

We started to head toward the stables when I heard that beautiful voice say, "Be careful of the black horse."

"They should know what the problems are here and why it is so important to have Silver Dash race," Uncle Ben said back to Mr. Johnson.

Uncle Ben looked back to us and explained, "Lucile had been winning for the past five years, which is how we were able to keep the stables going for as long as it has even though we have been having trouble paying off the loan."

"I mistakenly took out a loan that had twice the insurance rate than needed and have been trying to pay it off ever since I took it ten years ago. This year is supposed to be the year when I pay it off, but last year was really bad since Silver Dash didn't race, and we have been tight on out budget, which is why we haven't been able to upgrade the property lately," Mr. Johnson explained.

Now I understand why this is so important to them. The stables will close if we don't win the race, and Silver Dash is our best hope.

"I understand. We'll do our best," I said with enthusiasm.

"You can count on us," Josh said.

"Yeah, we'll help," Aliyah said.

"Thank you," Mr. Johnson said, sounding a bit relieved to hear it.

We started walking back to the stables until I heard a sound behind me. I looked back to see where it came from, but all I saw was Silver Dash staring at me while I held his reins. He nudged me to move on, and so I did. When we got back to the stables, I saw Johnny waiting for us. Uncle Ben called out to him, and we stopped to talk.

"Uncle Ben, one of the jockeys needs your help with a horse," Johnny said.

"I see. I'll go help them then. Johnson, can you help the kids find horses please?" Uncle Ben replied.

"No problem," Mr. Johnson said.

"Johnny, I want you to help Sara with Silver Dash," Uncle Ben said.

"Okay, Uncle Ben," Johnny replied and showed me the way to Silver Dash's stall.

While Aliyah, Josh, and Mr. Johnson were looking for horses, I untacked Silver Dash, which means I took the saddle and bridle off him. Silver Dash didn't want Johnny to touch him by flattening his ears back to his head and raising his head high above Johnny, basically saying he didn't want Johnny near him, so Johnny sat on a chair, watching me.

"Thanks anyway for the help, Johnny," I said.

"No problem. So you are going to run in the race on Friday?" Johnny asked.

"Yes. Uncle Ben says it will help Silver Dash and the stables," I answered.

"Do you know how to run in a real race?" Johnny asked.

"No. I've never ridden in a real race before," I answered.

"Would you like me to show you?" Johnny asked.

I looked at him and smiled. "Yes, please."

$$7$$

Johnny took me to one of the stalls where one of the horses was being tacked to run on the racetrack.

"This is Shining Star. She's been here for six years and has always run the Championship Race. She won one of the races but never won after Lucile came. That was the year when everyone met Lucile," Johnny said.

"Was she hired by Mr. Johnson?" I asked.

"No. She came here on her own and asked for a job. I don't know why, but Mr. Johnson was fine about hiring her. Anyway, I want you to see how the jockey rides when the horse is running," Johnny answered.

Johnny and I followed the jockey, a tall thin man wearing a dark-green-colored uniform, while he was leading Shining Star to the racetrack with a similar green blanket. The number on this one for Shining Star is the number nine in big bold white, which is also on the jockey's back. Johnny and I stayed at the railing to watch them run. The jockey mounted Shining Star and was ready to go.

"Watch carefully how the jockey makes Shining Star stay and then bolt out of the gate. You need to know how to act when the gate is opened," Johnny said.

The gate Johnny was talking about is the starting gate where all the racehorses are put into before they race. It allows all the horses to start off at the same time so no one gets a head start. The jockey was off the horse's back in his two-point position, ready to start running. The heels of his feet are down in the stirrups, and his hands are holding onto the reins. The jockey pushed his hands forward to give the horse the signal to run, and Shining Star ran just as the gate opened.

"The jockey gives the horse her head before the gate opens so that the horse knows to start running when it does. You have to do the same with Silver Dash at the starting gate. Now watch how the jockey moves his hands," Johnny said.

Johnny had brought a pair of binoculars for me to use in order to watch them in detail while they ran. The jockey was moving his hands back and forth with the horse's head, and the rest of his body was still and didn't move.

"You have to move with the horse's head so that he knows he can keep running. If you hold on to the reins and don't give the horse any of his head, he will slow down. That's what you were doing with Silver Dash earlier; you held on to his reins too tight while he was running. He can go faster than what he did before, but you held on to the reins and made him run slower," Johnny said.

"Did you learn all this just by watching, or did you learn it from your uncle?" I asked, amazed at how much Johnny knew about racing.

"Both. I learned most from my uncle, but I also learned different ways on how to ride by watching jockeys race," Johnny answered.

Just then, Aliyah and Josh came on to the track with two horses. They were each wearing jockey uniforms. Aliyah wore a lavender-colored one with the number seventeen on the back that matched the horse next to her. Josh wore a dark-orange color with the number nineteen on the back.

"Sara, look," Aliyah said, walking up to me. "This is Lucky Joe, and that one is Little John." She pointed to Josh's horse.

Lucky Joe was a beautiful white horse with a darker-white mane and tail. Little John was a paint, which is a type of color of a horse that has two different colors and looks like it was painted. The main colors are black, white, and brown, but there are many other variations of colors that can be considered "paint." His colors were brown and white. Little John was tall even though his name had "Little" in it. His mane and tail were also brown at the base and white at the end.

"We are going to ride them in the race," Aliyah said.

"Now hold on there," Mr. Johnson said.

Now that I think about it, there are a lot of "Johns" around here.

Anyway, Mr. Johnson continued, "First you two have to ride them so I can see if you are capable of riding a racehorse. Now mount up, and let's see if you two are good at riding like Sara said you were."

I giggled at that, and Aliyah mounted her horse. Aliyah went first while Josh held his off to the side, out of the way of the other people racing. She nudged Lucky Joe with her heels and started to run. Lucky Joe was fast, but I could tell he was nowhere near as fast as Silver Dash was. Aliyah looked like she was a pro at riding and was having fun. Mr. Johnson was impressed, and so was Johnny, who didn't run away this time. I was shocked at that.

When Aliyah came back, Josh mounted up. Aliyah dismounted and was out of breath. Mr. Johnson took Lucky Joe, and they went by the railing in order not to get in the way. Josh kicked Little John, and he reared up. Josh held on for his life, and then Little John took off. Josh almost fell but held on as Little John ran.

"I told that boy not to kick Little John. Does he ever listen?" Mr. Johnson asked.

"No," Aliyah and I answered at the same time and then laughed.

When Josh got back, he was still holding on to Little John for his life. I wanted to laugh real hard, but I held it in so I didn't embarrass him. Josh tried to get off Little John but fell off instead. Aliyah and I went to help Josh up while Johnny stayed back.

"Are you okay?" Aliyah asked.

"That was awesome!" Josh answered.

"He's okay," Aliyah and I said at the same time, looking at each other.

Mr. Johnson came up to Josh and said, "I told you not to kick the horse. If you do that again, I will not allow you to be in the race."

"Okay, sorry," Josh said with a guilty look on his face.

I looked around for Johnny, but he disappeared. I hoped he would get over this hiding game soon.

"Well, it looks like Aliyah can ride in the race. However, I'm not too sure about Josh," Mr. Johnson said.

"I can ride. Just give me another chance, and I'll show you that I can ride," Josh said, sounding determined.

Mr. Johnson sighed and said, "One more chance, but if you kick that horse again, I will look for another rider. Do you understand?"

"Yes, sir," Josh said, giving a mock salute.

"Now then, go clean these horses off, and we will call it a day," Mr. Johnson said.

We all went back to the stables until Johnny took my hand and pulled me back up against the side of the stable.

"Sara, you have to see this," Johnny said, a little out of breath.

Johnny took me back to the racetrack, but instead of being at the rail, we were hiding near a bench. I was about to ask what was going on when I saw Buck with Wild Night. Wild Night had a bridle and saddle on for riding. Buck had riding gear on and looked like he was actually going to ride Wild Night. His riding was the opposite of the one I wore, with most of the color being black with a white outline. He mounted Wild Night and was getting ready to run.

"Watch him," Johnny said, surprising me. "That's going to be your competition."

"What do you…?" I asked and then saw Wild Night run.

He was so fast that I could not believe it. He was a blur of motion as he looked like he could be as fast as Silver Dash. I was too mesmerized by what I saw.

"You and Silver Dash are going to be racing against them," Johnny said.

My mouth just dropped open when he said that.

8

When I slept that night, I had another dream about that beautiful-voiced lady who I was pretty sure was Lucile now.

She said, "Tell Silver Dash he has to run when you both race."

I did not understand what she meant by that, but I thought I would find out soon enough. He ran fine for me before, and he was going to run again. For some reason, it sounded like I was going to have to coax Silver Dash into running in the race. I didn't understand why I would have to do that if he likes running so much.

Johnny told me that Silver Dash and I have to work on running the racetrack properly until the Championship Race would start, so I got changed into my jockey uniform to practice running on the track with Silver Dash.

I went through my usual routine of brushing Silver Dash and tacking him, which to me felt like we were bonding even more now by being with each other.

I took Silver Dash out to the racetrack and saw Johnny, Uncle Ben, and Mr. Johnson waiting for me. Surprisingly, I did not see Aliyah or Josh there. I thought that they were still probably asleep because it was early in the morning. I mounted Silver Dash and got ready to run.

Uncle Ben came up to me and said, "Keep your elbows close to your sides, and move with Silver Dash's head when he runs."

"Okay," I said, both feeling nervous and excited about running again. I never got over how fast Silver Dash could run, but I'm not worried about falling off. I tried to think of other things to get my mind focused instead of thinking about the dream I had.

"Whenever you are ready, Sara, you can run," Uncle Ben said.

I focused my mind on moving my hands with Silver Dash's head to calm myself with a tingle of anxiousness running up my spine. I go into my two-point position, put my heels down in the stirrups, and gave Silver Dash his head just like the jockey on Shining Star did.

When I did that, Silver Dash started running so fast I felt like I was tipping sideways off him. Once I righted myself, I tried to focus on Silver Dash's head moving, but it was moving too fast for me. I could not watch because I was getting dizzy and I couldn't keep up with all the movement. Instead, I closed my eyes for the brief moment of relief I needed and tried to feel what Silver Dash was doing under me to try and get my bearings since everything was rushing by in a blur too fast for my brain to process.

I was too shocked at how fast we were soaring through the track more so than the first time we ran. We were truly flying, and I felt weightless in the saddle while trying to concentrate on Silver Dash moving.

I read in a book once that if you can concentrate on how the horse is moving, you can feel what he's doing as well, so I concentrated on what Silver Dash was doing underneath me, and I could feel him. I could feel how fast his legs were moving and even know which lead he was in. The lead is when the horse's front hoof starts to run, like he either starts running with his right front hoof or his left front hoof.

Silver Dash started with his left front hoof, which was the wrong lead. The horse should start running with the hoof that is closer to the rail. We were closer to the right rail, but I couldn't worry about that for now. I also started feeling Silver Dash's head move in a steady rhythm.

Yes, we were moving fast, but Silver Dash had a pace of his own once he started moving that I didn't feel before. After concentrating hard enough on his movements, I was able to finally feel his rhythm.

Once I could feel his movements better, I opened my eyes again and moved my hands with his head so he could go faster, and he did. Moving my hands with his head had him running so fast like we were soaring above the racetrack. His legs are strong and moving so fast that I could not feel them, which it felt like we were soaring in the air, flying like a bird high in the sky with nothing stopping us.

After a bit of running and things started to clear a bit, even though everything was a still a blur around me, I felt pain and saw nothing. Blackness took me and I could hear people talking, but I could not understand them.

I think I fell off.

When I opened my eyes and they cleared from a blurry haze, I see Silver Dash looking down at me, his gray snout on my head and his dark-blue eyes asking why I'm lying on the ground. Uncle Ben and Johnny are looking at me, sitting next to me and talking. Johnny said something, but I could not hear him—all I had was ringing in my ears. Then someone picked me up off the ground. Mr. Johnson was the one who picked me up, and Silver Dash nuzzled me to make sure I was okay. I pet Silver Dash and told him I was okay, but when I tried to stand, I felt all the pain of falling off a horse.

My entire body hurt—my legs, arms, back, shoulders, chest, head, everything hurt. All I could feel was numbness, and Mr. Johnson had to help me walk. I kept saying I was okay, but I still could not hear what they were saying past the buzzing in my ears.

I think I called out to Silver Dash to follow, but Uncle Ben was already leading him with the reins. I remember Aliyah and Josh coming over to see me, and they looked worried. Everything that happened after that, I forgot because I fell asleep and didn't wake up until later in the evening.

When I woke up, Aliyah was sitting in a chair next to me, and I was in my room on the bed.

"I'm so glad you're awake, Sara. Are you okay? Do you feel any better?" Aliyah said.

"A little bit." I answered. "What happened?"

"You fell off Silver Dash when he was running really fast. Mr. Johnson said Silver Dash was at his top speed of forty miles an hour. He said you were lucky you didn't break any bones. The sand and your helmet saved you. The helmet cracked in the back because you fell head first. All you have are a few cuts and bruises. Your nose and lip were bleeding, but it was not serious. You're really lucky," Aliyah answered.

My head was hurting, so I put my hand on it. "How did I fall?" I asked.

"I don't know. Uncle Ben said you looked to the side, lost your reins, and one of your feet came out of the stirrup. When your foot came out of the stirrup, you fell sideways, hitting your head first, and rolled. He said that Silver Dash stopped running and went to check on you. Silver Dash was really worried about you," Aliyah answered.

I smiled when she said that. I felt happy for a minute thinking Silver Dash liked me a lot, but then I remembered that he thinks that I was Lucile and not me.

"When I feel better, I have to show him that I'm all right," I said.

"You have to show everyone that you're all right. Mr. Johnson, Uncle Ben, and Johnny were all worried about you—Josh the most. He came in every hour to see how you were doing," Aliyah added.

I smiled and felt like I was blushing.

"Really?" I asked.

Aliyah smiled, and I knew I was blushing now.

*****

When I felt good enough to get out of bed, Aliyah and I went to the stables to see Silver Dash first. When we got there, I saw Mr. Johnson, Uncle Ben, Johnny, and Josh near Silver Dash's stable. When they all saw me, they smiled and walked toward me.

Josh walked really fast and asked, "Are you okay, Sara"?

I smiled and answered back, "I'm fine. I just have a headache."

"Let's be glad that's all you have. You are very lucky, Sara. That fall could have broken a bone or two. Not many people come out of those falls with just a headache," Mr. Johnson said.

Uncle Ben gave a glance at Mr. Johnson and looked a little angry.

"We are all very happy that you are feeling all right," Uncle Ben said.

Now Johnny looked a little angry, and so did Josh.

I got the feeling they were all hiding something from me, so I asked, "Is there something you guys are not telling me"?

They looked at each other, and I looked at Aliyah. She didn't know what was going on either.

"Mr. Johnson decided to take you out of the race," Johnny said.

"What?" Aliyah and I yelled.

9

"What do you mean you're taking me out of the race?" I asked angrily.

"You can't take her out of the race. Who is going to ride Silver Dash other than Sara? Who is going to save the stables?" Aliyah said angrily, understanding my feelings.

"I have already decided!" Mr. Johnson said in a loud voice.

"It is better for you, Sara. We don't want you to get hurt again," Uncle Ben said.

"What about Silver Dash? What's going to happen to him? What's going to happen to the stables?" I asked, worried.

"Silver Dash will retire from racing and live the rest of his life grazing on grass fields. As for the stables, it will have to shut down," Mr. Johnson said and walked away.

I didn't even have time to argue with him. Uncle Ben left with Mr. Johnson. Johnny and Josh stayed with Aliyah and I though.

"I'm sorry, Sara," Johnny said.

"No, it's okay Johnny," I said.

I didn't feel like talking because I was so surprised at what Mr. Johnson said. I walked over to Silver Dash's stall. Silver Dash saw me and walked up to me. I opened the stall because I wanted to hug Silver Dash. When I opened the stall, Silver Dash put his nose right up to my face. I held his nose and started to cry. Aliyah, Josh, and Johnny went up next to me and put their hands on my shoulders to comfort me.

When I was done crying, I went to my room. I told Aliyah that I wanted to be alone so I could think. Only I just wanted to sleep because I got even more of a headache than when I woke up. I was lying down on my bed, just thinking about everything that happened. I mean after all that work and riding I did, I felt that I should be in the race. I couldn't understand how I fell off Silver Dash.

I tried to think about what happened. I remembered riding Silver Dash and closing my eyes to feel his movements. I tried to remember the fall. I couldn't think—it was almost like it never happened.

Even though I couldn't remember, my body did. I tried to think of what happened after I opened my eyes. It was just a blur. I could not remember anything about the fall. What I wanted to do was go back to the track to see if something there would help me remember.

I read a book that said if something "traumatic" happened to a person, their brain will forget the event to protect the person. "Traumatic" incidents are when something bad or scary happened to you like a fall or a car crash. The book also said that if people who forget the "traumatic" event wish to remember it, then they could go to where it happened, and it might jog their memory.

That's what I'll do.

I got up from my bed and went to Silver Dash's stall. He came up to me to check on me. No one was around except for all the horses. I felt that if I brought Silver Dash with me, he could help me remember what happened. I opened Silver Dash's stall, took a lead line, and attached it to his halter. We walked to the racetrack until I saw Uncle Ben and Mr. Johnson standing near the rail. I looked around for a hiding spot so they would not see me, and then I looked at Silver Dash. I tried to think how I was going to hide him when he's so big.

There looked like a big-enough space to hide Silver Dash under the bleachers where lots of people sit to watch horse races.

I said, "Silver Dash, come here," and we walked in.

There was an opening where I could be close to Uncle Ben and Mr. Johnson to hear what they were talking about. I looked out the opening and saw them right in front of me. The opening was too small for them to see me, so I just waited until they started talking. I didn't mean to eavesdrop, but I also didn't want them to find me with Silver Dash after what happened.

Silver Dash put his head on my shoulder, and we listened to what Uncle Ben and Mr. Johnson were taking about.

"I don't care what the horse needs. I'm not putting her back on him," Mr. Johnson said angrily.

"Lucile's final words to us were to let Silver Dash run. The only way for that to happen is for a rider to ride him," Uncle Ben said back angrily.

"What if she breaks a bone or something worse happens? I couldn't live with myself if another person died like Lucile did. I don't care if I lose the stables," Mr. Johnson said.

"Sara is the only person who can ride Silver Dash besides Lucile. Sara was lucky, yes. I couldn't forgive myself if something happens to her as well, but this is what happens to riders all the time. They know the dangers of riding in a race like this," Uncle Ben said.

"I'm not letting Sara back on Silver Dash. I'm too worried about her," Mr. Johnson said.

So he was really worried about me. I wanted to go hug him for saying that. I didn't know he cared about me that much. I started to understand why he didn't want me in the race now, but I still wasn't going to give up.

"At least give her another chance. It is wrong for us to make her go through all this training and suddenly take it away from her," Uncle Ben said.

"Yes, it is wrong. It is wrong to put her on that horse. It is wrong to make her go through training and put pressure on her to try and save the stables. It is wrong to think that she could be like Lucile," Mr. Johnson said, sounding so sad it broke my heart.

Silence stretched for a few moments.

"I'm sorry about Lucile, Johnson. She was the perfect daughter to have," Uncle Ben said.

Wait! Lucile was his daughter?

I almost fell over if it wasn't for Silver Dash standing behind me. I was starting to understand everything, but I couldn't help feeling that it was because of how much I look like Lucile. They were hoping I was exactly like Lucile and forgot that I'm Sara, so Mr. Johnson was feeling guilty for how he had been acting.

"I can't stop thinking about it. Why did I not check the track that morning? Why did she have to die?" Mr. Johnson said and started to cry.

I started to feel sorry for him now, but I can't be Lucile. I only look like her, so I can't be his daughter whom he misses so much. Uncle Ben tried to comfort Mr. Johnson. They both left the track, going back to the stables.

Mr. Johnson stopped crying, but Uncle Ben still tried to comfort him by putting his hand on Mr. Johnson's shoulder. When they were both out of sight, Silver Dash and I headed for the track. I didn't hold Silver Dash's lead line because I knew he wouldn't walk away from me.

I couldn't remember where I fell, so I stood in the middle of the track and looked around. I turned around, looked at the sand, looked at the rails, but nothing was helping. I couldn't remember the fall.

"Silver Dash, I just can't remember what happened," I said.

Silver Dash looked at the track and trotted off.

"Silver Dash, wait!" I yelled after him.

I started to run after him. I didn't know what he was doing or why he trotted off, but somehow I knew he was trying to help. Silver Dash stopped by some bushes near the rail. When I got there, I didn't see anything.

"Silver Dash, what is it?" I asked.

Silver Dash nudged the bushes to move them, and I saw something shining. I helped Silver Dash move the trees and saw a metal rod. I picked it up, and my head started to hurt. I put my hand to my head and started to remember someone swing the metal rod at me.

Then I looked at Silver Dash, and I remembered that I was riding Silver Dash when it happened. While I was riding Silver Dash, I looked sideways and saw someone swing the metal rod at me. I remembered moving sideways to miss getting hit, and that's when I fell.

"Silver Dash, we have to go tell Uncle Ben and Mr. Johnson," I said and took Silver Dash's lead line to walk back to the stables with the metal rod in my hand.

10

When Silver Dash and I got back to the stables, I saw Aliyah and Josh looking worried. When they saw me, they ran toward me.

"Sara, are you okay?" Aliyah asked, worried. "We've been looking all over for you."

"I'm sorry, you guys. I didn't mean to scare you like that," I answered.

"Why are you holding that metal rod, Sara?" Josh asked, his brow furrowing in confusion.

"Yeah, and why do you have Silver Dash with you?" Aliyah asked.

I looked at Silver Dash and then at the metal rod.

"I have to talk to Uncle Ben and Mr. Johnson. Did you guys see them?" I asked.

"Yeah. We told them you went missing, and they got worried, so they went to look for you," Aliyah answered.

"Go find them and tell them I'm here. I have to tell all of you something important," I said, and Aliyah and Josh ran away to find Uncle Ben and Mr. Johnson.

I put Silver Dash back in his stall and waited for everyone to come, laying my back against the stall door. I stared at the metal rod and tried to remember who the person was, but I couldn't remember. Aliyah and Josh came back a few minutes later with Uncle Ben and Mr. Johnson running toward me.

"Where have you been? We were all worried!" Mr. Johnson said angrily.

He was probably worried the most, which kind of made me feel special in a way. I'll tell him that I overheard their conversation and tell him not to feel so guilty anymore about it.

"I couldn't remember the fall so I wanted to find out what happened. I went to the track with Silver Dash," I said, and Mr. Johnson looked like he was about to yell.

"Now don't freak out just yet because I found out why I fell," I said quickly before Mr. Johnson could yell.

Now everyone looked confused, but at least they let me speak.

"While I was riding Silver Dash, I saw someone swing this metal rod at me, and that's why I fell," I said and held up the metal rod.

"What?" Aliyah and Josh said at the same time.

"Are you sure of this, Sara?" Uncle Ben asked.

"Yes, I remember seeing someone swing it at me, and I tried to move away from getting hit, but I fell off of Silver Dash instead," I answered.

"Let me see that rod," Mr. Johnson said, and I give it to him. He looked at it with a puzzled expression. "I don't know who would have tried to hurt you, but it's obvious that they don't want you in this race. This is even more of a reason why you shouldn't ride. You are not going to ride in this race. That's final!" Mr. Johnson said then stormed out of the stables, but I wasn't going to give up that easily and ran after him.

When I got close to him, I yelled, "Wait, Mr. Johnson!"

He stopped and turned to say something, but I stopped him before he could say anything once I got close to look up at him.

"I heard what you and Uncle Ben were talking about by the track," I said loudly.

I didn't know that Aliyah, Josh, and Uncle Ben came and were listening, but it was too late to take it back.

"I know that Lucile was your daughter, and I'm really sorry for you," I said loudly again because I needed him to listen to me.

I could see the surprise and sadness in his face. His eyes had started to water too.

"I also know that you've been thinking of me as your daughter too—or more that you wanted me to be like her, like Lucile." I started to lower my voice because I realized how loud I was. "You can't think of me as Lucile because I'm not her. I may look like her, but I'm not her. I'm sorry that she died, but you don't have to worry about me. I'm just a student who came to see horse racing. However, I know deep down that Lucile would not be mad at you for what happened. I wouldn't want you to feel guilty if I was your daughter. You don't have to feel guilty for something that wasn't your fault. It was a terrible accident that no one could have stopped."

I saw Mr. Johnson's shoulders moving as he put a hand over his eyes. I knew he was crying, so I hugged him as hard as I could. He wrapped me in his arms and sobbed quietly. After a couple minutes, he let go and stared down at me.

"I'm sorry, Sara. I didn't mean to get you involved in all of this. I was so devastated about Lucile's death that I put all the pressure on you. You shouldn't have to deal with my personal matters. I'm sorry for everything and for thinking that you could be like Lucile. I had kept Lucile a secret from the other jockeys so as not to show favoritism, so I told them that she was a good rider and could win. She wanted to help save the stables just as much as you do. That's why I thought you to be Lucile," Mr. Johnson said, wiping his face with a napkin that he had in shirt pocket.

"Well, it seems like everything is better now," Uncle Ben said.

"Lucile was your daughter, Mr. Johnson?" Aliyah asked.

I said "oops" in my head and was worried I embarrassed Mr. Johnson. I looked up at him, but he was smiling now.

"Yes, she was," Mr. Johnson answered.

"I'm sorry for your loss," Aliyah said.

"Thank you," Mr. Johnson replied.

"So, what now?" Josh asked.

"What do you mean, Josh?" Aliyah asked.

"I mean, what about the race? Is Sara going to race or not?" Josh asked.

Everyone looked at Josh and then at Mr. Johnson. I looked at Mr. Johnson, and he looked back at me. He stared at me for a few long moments with a serious expression on his face.

"I don't like that someone was trying to hurt you, but I can't have Lucile be mad at me for not letting Silver Dash race," Mr. Johnson said with determination in his voice now.

Then I smiled back at him. Aliyah and Josh yelled "yea" and hugged each other. Then they looked at each other and pushed away with awkward expressions, which made me laugh out loud.

"Well, we have a lot of work to do. The race is in four days, so everyone needs to get in as much practicing as they can," Mr. Johnson said.

Everyone headed upstairs for a good night's sleep. When I went started up the stairs, I saw Johnny around the corner.

"What's wrong, Sara?" Aliyah asked.

"Nothing, I was thinking of saying good night to Silver Dash. I'll meet you upstairs," I answered.

Everyone went upstairs to their rooms, and Johnny came out.

"Were you here this whole time?" I asked Johnny.

"Yeah, I was, and I'm happy you will be able to race," Johnny answered.

"Wow, I didn't even see you," I said.

"I'm good at hiding," Johnny said back.

"Johnny, are you shy around people?" I asked because it had been bothering me that he was always hiding every time there was a crowd.

Johnny looked away, and I could see a blush on his cheeks. *Yep—he's shy around people.*

"The reason I lied about being sick is because I really do get nervous around so many people that I was sure I would get sick if I was in a bus full of people. Uncle Ben knows about it and tries to help, but it's hard sometimes to work through it," he replies.

"I'm sure one day you'll be able to get through it," I said.

"I wanted to warn you. It was Buck who tried to hurt you," Johnny said after a moment.

"You saw him?" I asked.

"Yeah, but I couldn't stop him. I wanted to apologize for not stopping him and letting you get hurt," Johnny answered, looking really sad about it.

"How did you know he was there?" I asked.

"In order to hide from everyone, I go to a small part of the track where there are bushes so that I can watch without people seeing me.

I was there watching you, and I heard someone come up behind me, so I moved before they saw me. When I looked back, I saw that it was Buck, and he had that metal rod. I didn't realize what he was doing until it was too late and he swung at you. When he missed, he ran away," Johnny answered.

"It's okay, Johnny. You didn't know he was going to do that. Besides, I'll just beat him in the race instead," I said, trying to cheer him up.

Johnny nodded at me, and we headed upstairs for the night.

Nothing crazy happened for the next few days while Aliyah, Josh, and I practiced riding for the race. The only problem was Josh constantly complaining about his butt being sore all the time. Aliyah and I were used to riding since we went to the same riding club back home. We were getting better at it. Josh took two days to really get the hang of riding while Aliyah and I improved our riding styles. I was also getting used to how fast Silver Dash could run. I was doing better at finding his rhythm and concentrating on how we soared through the track, our timing getting better and better.

I told Aliyah, Josh, Mr. Johnson, and Uncle Ben about it—what Johnny had said about Buck trying to hit me. Mr. Johnson said he would go find Buck while Uncle Ben tried to find Johnny, but they could not find either of them. Johnny came a few times to talk to me but didn't stay too long. He seemed really nervous with his uncle constantly trying to find him.

While I was practicing on our last day before the Championship Race, Aliyah and Josh were watching me behind the rail. They were talking, but I could not make out what they were talking about because it was always hard to clearly see anything while Silver Dash ran so fast.

When we went around the track again, I saw Mr. Johnson and Uncle Ben talking to Aliyah and Josh. I thought about slowing Silver Dash down so I could talk to Mr. Johnson and Uncle Ben, but I didn't want to stop Silver Dash from soaring around the track. I always felt like I was flying when Silver Dash runs, and I loved the feeling.

After another few minutes of running, I slowed Silver Dash down to a halt next to everyone.

"What's going on?" I asked.

"We still have not been able to find Buck or Johnny yet," Uncle Ben answered. "Usually Johnny is fine with coming out. He never sneaks around this much. I'm getting worried about him."

"Maybe it's because we are here," Aliyah said, gesturing to herself and Josh.

"Yeah, he's always been nervous around people from school," Josh agreed.

"He's never been nervous around me," Uncle Ben insisted.

"Well, that's because you're his uncle, Uncle Ben," Aliyah said.

I giggled at that because it was funny to hear "uncle" said twice in a row.

"It's okay, Uncle Ben. When Johnny comes to talk to me, I'll tell him you are worried and want to talk," I said.

"Why does Johnny only come out to talk to you, Sara?" Aliyah asked.

"Maybe it's because he likes you," Josh said with a grumpy expression. That was odd because I couldn't figure out why he was upset.

Aliyah looked at him with a weird face that I couldn't understand. *Does she know something?*

"No," I said with a confused tone. "He talks to me because I was the one who saw him when we first got here. He didn't want anyone to know that he was here after he got in trouble."

"Anyway, we will talk about this matter later," Mr. Johnson said and pointed a finger at me. "You have to practice more. The race is tomorrow, and you have to be ready for it."

Silver Dash got all excited after he heard that. He never lost energy, that's for sure. So I went into my two-point position, pressed in my legs, and Silver Dash took off.

After the training, we all went back to the stables. I was untacking Silver Dash while everyone else was getting ready for dinner. Then Johnny came out of nowhere.

"Hey, Johnny," I said when he walked up to me.

"Thanks for sticking up for me earlier," Johnny said.

I was a little confused at first, and then I thought that he was probably there watching us like always.

"Of course, but you should really talk to your uncle. He's getting worried, and I think he's upset about you avoiding him constantly. You can't always hide from everyone. You will never be able to get friends or have fun in your life. Sooner or later, you are going to have to come out and face the world," I said.

Johnny just stared at me when I said that. Ever heard of an awkward silence? That's what it was with Johnny staring at me. Silver Dash whinnied, and I jumped in surprise. I guess Silver Dash didn't like the silence either.

I pet him and said to Johnny, "Anyway, you should go talk to your uncle. Please at least tell him why you are so shy. Maybe he can help."

"I know, but I just don't know what to say," Johnny replied.

"Just tell him the truth. I think that is all he wants from you. Just tell him what you told me. There is nothing to be afraid of. He's your family," I said, encouraging him.

Then Johnny smiled! I had never seen Johnny smile before. He had a nice genuine smile, almost as if he just wanted someone to tell him that "there is nothing to be afraid of."

"You're right. I'll go talk to Uncle Ben. Thank you, Sara," Johnny said.

I smiled and said, "You're welcome."

Johnny left, and I finished taking care of Silver Dash. I went to go eat dinner and thought about what was going to happen tomorrow.

That night, I dreamed of Lucile again, and her voice was getting foggier each night I had dreamed of her. Sometimes I could tell what she was saying, and other times it was her saying to let Silver Dash run.

This time, I only heard a little bit of what she said to me: "Look for…don't let him…Dash…before you cross…"

Then I woke up.

12

The Championship Race was here—the day I would ride Silver Dash in a real race and finally become a jockey. I felt so excited and nervous at the same time. I felt like I could not stand still and wanted to get on the racetrack as soon as possible. However, it was only morning.

I felt so excited that I quickly got dressed and ran down to the stables to see Silver Dash. I didn't know what time it was, and the race started at noon. I went to see Silver Dash, and he was excited just like I was. I think he knew it was race day. Aliyah came running toward me.

"Sara, no!" Aliyah said loudly.

Now I'm confused. What did I do?

"Sara, you have to rest more before the race," Aliyah said, grabbing my arm and pulling me toward the stairs.

I pulled back and said, "I'm too excited to rest, Aliyah. I want to get Silver Dash ready."

"Do you know what time it is?" Aliyah asked.

I thought for a minute and shook my head. "No."

"It's eight in the morning. You still have four hours left to rest," Aliyah answered.

I usually don't get up so early, but I guess I was too excited. I couldn't believe it was only eight.

"I'm up and dressed already. I can't go back to sleep," I said with enthusiasm.

Then I just realized that Aliyah was also dressed. She usually doesn't wake up until eleven. She sleeps for the longest time. One time she slept until two in the afternoon. She can sleep forever if she wanted to.

I narrowed my eyes at her, and she just puffed out her chest, noticing I figured out she was also as excited as I am.

"At least eat something. You can't go riding on an empty stomach," Aliyah said, pulling me toward the dining room this time.

"Okay, Mom," I joked.

Then Aliyah gave me a scary face, and I giggled.

Aliyah smiled and said in a surprisingly motherly tone, "You have to eat all your vegetables."

Then we both laughed and ate breakfast. Surprisingly, Josh was not here. I asked Aliyah where he was, and she said that he was practicing for the race one last time. Josh never gets up so early. He's as bad as Aliyah when it comes to sleeping. I guess everyone's excited for the race.

After breakfast, Aliyah and I headed out to check on Josh. We got to the railing and found Uncle Ben and Mr. Johnson watching Josh.

"He has improved since last time," Mr. Johnson said.

"He actually got better?" Aliyah asked, surprised. "That's a first."

I giggled, but it was true. Josh doesn't get better at something unless it was important to him, so this must be really important to him.

"Well, he's getting better at riding and going around the turn. Are you excited, Sara?" Uncle Ben asked.

"Yes, I am," I answered, but then I suddenly felt overwhelmed because I just realized that this was my first real race.

"I'm also nervous. This is my first race on an actual racetrack. There are going to be people watching me on the stands," I said, really nervous now.

"Don't worry, Sara. You will be fine. Silver Dash knows how to race. All you have to do is hold on. Don't get nervous with people watching you either. Just feel Silver Dash under you, and think of flying like you always do. I know you will do great," Mr. Johnson said.

I smiled, and Mr. Johnson smiled back.

"Thank you, Mr. Johnson," I said.

"You're welcome, Sara," Mr. Johnson said back.

Josh was done running and came over to us. Little John looked ready for the race.

"How did I do?" Josh asked Uncle Ben.

Uncle Ben was holding a stopwatch in his hand and looked at it.

"Better than your last run. I think you are ready for the race. All of you are ready, and it should be a fine race today," Uncle Ben said.

Time flew by, and it was eleven now. I had already changed into the jockey uniform I wore before—the white uniform with black lining that Mr. Johnson had given me when I first rode Silver Dash. What surprised me the most was when Mr. Johnson told me it was Lucile's race uniform. I had a feeling it was, but I didn't want to be excited about it if it wasn't. He said it looked good on me and he wanted me to wear it for the race.

I was tacking Silver Dash up with his saddle and bridle. The blanket matched the number one on my back. He was excited, constantly scraping his hoof on the ground, wanting to go outside. When I was finished tacking Silver Dash up, Johnny came over from behind the corner.

"Hey, Johnny, how did it go with your uncle?" I asked.

"It went well. I told him the truth like you said, and he was happy about that. What he really wanted to talk about was if I was hurt. He thought that I might have gotten hurt by Buck since I saw him," Johnny answered.

I was too shocked for words. Johnny was happy that his uncle was worried about him. Then I smiled and said, "I'm glad he wasn't angry at you."

"Yeah, I was shocked too. I really thought he was angry with me," Johnny said.

"Are you going to watch the race?" I asked.

"Yes, and I'm not going to hide this time. I'm going to watch you with my uncle near the railing," Johnny answered.

"I'm glad," I said.

Johnny and I walked together with Silver Dash to a place near the track where they keep all the horses before they start the race. There were separate spaces with wall ties on them for every horse. There were many horses from other stables with their riders and trainers together. There was a stall for Silver Dash, so I brought him there. I hooked him up and looked for Uncle Ben and Mr. Johnson, but they weren't around anywhere.

"I'll go look for my uncle and find out where everyone is," Johnny said as he ran off.

I looked around to see all the different horses. There were pure-white horses with white manes and tails, painted horses that were both black and white, chestnut-colored horses with creamy -colored manes and tails; I could keep going on and on. There were at least a dozen horses that were competing, and I started to feel nervous again. Then Silver Dash nudged me as if he knew how I was feeling, so I smiled and pet his nose.

"You're right. I shouldn't be worried since I have you," I said and hugged Silver Dash.

Then Mr. Johnson came running over.

"Sorry, Sara. I was helping Aliyah get her horse tacked up. She is going to race first, and if she gets in at third place, then Josh will race. As long as Josh gets third place in his race, you will be able to race Silver Dash in the final round," Mr. Johnson said, excited.

"I know Aliyah and Josh will win," I said, but I was still feeling nervous. I couldn't calm down with all the excitement of the race and because of my dream.

What was Lucile trying to tell me?

Two hours passed. Aliyah had won second place in her race, and Josh was in the middle of his. I was waiting for the announcement of the race to finish and hear who had won. The announcer said two names, and I was starting to worry that maybe Josh didn't make it, but then I heard Josh's name be called for third place.

I was so happy that I hugged Mr. Johnson and then Silver Dash and said, "We are going to race. I can't believe it."

"Get ready then," Mr. Johnson said.

I took a few deep breaths and nodded at Mr. Johnson. He gave me a leg up on to Silver Dash. He walked Silver Dash with a lead line to the track near the starting gates. He then said good luck to me, took off the lead line, and let Silver Dash go.

There were only six racehorses for the final race, and one of them was pure black. It was Wild Night with Buck riding him, which surprised me since everyone had been looking for him for the past few days. Buck looked at me with an angry face, and I looked back at him with an equally angry one. Silver Dash picked up his foot and scratched the ground three times. I could tell he wanted to race against Wild Night.

Wild Night whinnied, and Buck tugged on the reins to move him away from us. I pulled Silver Dash over to keep him away from Wild Night. All the horses are put into the numbered gates that matched each horse. Silver Dash is put in first because we were number one.

Once all the horses were in the gates, everyone in the stands went silent. Silver Dash was excited to run. The silence was loud, and there was a ringing in my ears. I got in my two-point position, took a deep breath, and closed my eyes to concentrate on Silver Dash. I opened my eyes, ready when the gates opened and Silver Dash bolts into gallop. I gave Silver Dash his head and moved my arms with his head so he could run as fast as he could.

All my training the past few days conditioned my body for this race, and it was easy to get into a rhythm. All I heard was people screaming in the stands in the background while the rest of the world turned to a blur. Silver Dash ran faster and faster, leaving the other horses behind except for Wild Night.

Wild Night was running just as fast as we were. I was too surprised that another horse was as fast as Silver Dash was. Everything was already blurring together, so I could tell we were soaring across the racetrack. I kept looking at Buck and at Silver Dash's head, all while staying in my two-point position and moving my hands with Silver Dash's head to keep him running fast. It was not easy trying to concentrate on so many things while my muscles started to burn.

A normal type of horse race has a certain length for horses to run in a one loop track. This track was a smaller type of track, which meant we had to do three full circles to win. I was pretty sure we already passed our first lap and running our second. Wild Night was still next to us, and I couldn't think of what to do.

How can we beat them when he is just as fast as us?

Then the dream from last night came back to me suddenly. The voice in my head became clearer and said, "Look for the black horse, and don't let him run next to Silver Dash when you race. Remind him to run for himself before you cross the finish line, and you will see how he can soar."

I remembered the time I fell off Silver Dash when he ran at his top speed, so I did what I did last time. I pressed my legs into Silver Dash and gave him as much of his head as I could and let him run.

Suddenly we start running past Wild Night and running faster and faster and faster. Everything went silent around me. The wind was the only thing I heard while the world moved so fast that all I felt was Silver Dash and I becoming the wind itself and soaring in the sky.

At the last turn, we were running straight for the finish line with a pole near the inside of the rail to show the winner.

Suddenly a shadowy figure appeared in front of us at the finish line. The figure turned into the shape of woman in a jockey uniform as she became easier to see. More details start to appear around her, and I could see that she looked just like me. Silver Dash picked up his head a bit and his ears twitched and I could feel it inside me somehow that he could also see the woman too. I realized that it was Lucile.

Lucile put her hands out in front of her and said in an angelic voice that we should not have been able to hear but could, "Come, Silver Dash, run, my sweet boy."

Somehow, when it should not have been possible, Silver Dash picked up speed and ran even faster than he ever had before. We passed the finish line and ran through Lucile.

For a second, it was white. I was not on Silver Dash or running on the track. Instead, it felt like I was in the air on a bed of clouds. Lucile appeared in front of me.

"Thank you, Sara. Thank you for letting Silver Dash race. He needed to run. Tell him I love him. He won't need me anymore," Lucile said.

Then she disappeared before I could say anything. The world came back into focus, and I was on Silver Dash passing the finish line with people screaming in the stands. I slowed Silver Dash to a halt and dismounted. He looked at me and I looked at him and somehow I knew that he no longer saw me as Lucile but as me.

"She said she loves you," I told him, and he nudged me into a hug.

Aliyah and Josh came running over with Johnny, Uncle Ben, and Mr. Johnson right behind them. Aliyah and Josh hugged me so tight that it hurts, but I didn't care as I hugged them both.

"You did it! You won!" Aliyah yelled over the crowd.

"Yeah," I said and looked back over at Silver Dash. "We won."

Silver Dash and I were brought over to the winner's circle where they put a rose blanket on Silver Dash and gave me the Championship Cup. It looked just like Lucile's, but it had this day's date on it along with my name. A man took a picture of all of us. Silver Dash and I were in the middle while Aliyah, Josh, and Johnny were on my left side and Uncle Ben and Mr. Johnson were on Silver Dash's right side. I held up the Championship Cup, and Silver Dash put his nose to it while the man took the picture.

Epilogue

A week passed since the Championship Cup. Silver Dash was outside, eating grass next to the fence, while Aliyah, Josh, and I were sitting on the fence, enjoying the warm weather and cloudless sky. We all decided to stay at Crest Hill Stables for the summer and worked on the ranch.

After the race, Mr. Johnson had called the police to arrest Buck for attacking me. Wild Night was put into retirement and given to a very nice ranch farm that specializes in taking care of aggressive horses. Mr. Johnson had said that Buck thought he would be able to win the race and get the prize money this year since Silver Dash wasn't going to race. He wanted to scare me enough not to run in the race so he could win by trying to injure me.

Unfortunately for him, I didn't scare easy, and he was locked up now. I told Mr. Johnson to hold on to the prize money since I didn't want it and that he could use it to pay off the debt he owed and fix up some parts of the stables that were starting to go bad. Needless to say, he was so happy that he cried again while hugging me.

"So, Josh, do you like Sara?" Aliyah said all of sudden, breaking the calm quiet we were in.

I could feel my face turning red, and Josh looked away.

"Aliyah!" I yelled with a squeaked voice.

"It's finally time we find out. Josh, do you like Sara? Yes or no?" Aliyah said, looking very hard at Josh.

Josh was still looking away, and I could see his ears turning red. He mumbled something I couldn't hear, his neck turning red now.

"What was that? We couldn't hear you?" Aliyah said, trying to look Josh in the face. He kept turning his body away from her, but it wasn't working. Aliyah was getting closer and closer to him without giving him any space.

"What?" Aliyah said louder.

Josh finally jumped off the fence and turned around to face us.

"I like her, okay!" Josh yelled at the top of his lungs, which echoed all around us.

His face was completely beet red, but he never looked away from me. I could feel my face burning, but I didn't look away either. Aliyah, however, had a big bright smile on her face watching the show.

"I like you too, Josh," I said in a soft voice.

"What was that, Sara? That was really low, and I couldn't hear you," Aliyah said, taunting me.

"I said I really like Josh too!" I yelled at the top of my voice, which echoed just like before.

"Good—that's all I wanted to know," Aliyah said, jumping down off the fence, and walked away with a skip. Silver Dash just kept eating grass and ignored our awkwardness.

Josh and I just looked at each other for what felt like forever but were probably just a few seconds.

"Well, what now?" I asked, breaking the awkward silence.

Josh blinked a few times and then held out his hand to me. "I think that makes us boyfriend and girlfriend now," he said with a shy smile on his face.

I smiled back and took Josh's hand, saying, "Yeah, I think it does."

We followed Aliyah back to the stables hand in hand, our fingers twinging together while Silver Dash joined us.

The End

www.ingramcontent.com/pod-product-compliance
Lightning Source LLC
Chambersburg PA
CBHW071951190726
48293CB00004B/1434